Wemberly Worried

17020l

KEVIN HENKES

GREENWILLOW BOOKS

An Imprint of HarperCollins*Publishers*

For Phyllis, who never worries

Watercolor paints and a black pen
were used for the full-color art.
The text type is Usherwood.

Wemberly Worried
Copyright © 2000 by Kevin Henkes
All rights reserved.
Printed in Hong Kong by South China
Printing Company (1988) Ltd.
www.harperchildrens.com

Library of Congress Cataloging-in-Publication Data

Henkes, Kevin.
Wemberly worried / by Kevin Henkes.
    p.   cm.
"Greenwillow Books."
Summary: A mouse named Wemberly,
who worries about everything, finds that
she has a whole list of things to worry
about when she faces the first day of
nursery school.
ISBN 0-688-17027-7 (trade)
ISBN 0-688-17028-5 (lib. bdg.)
[1. Worry—Fiction.   2. First day
of school—Fiction.   3. Nursery
schools—Fiction.   4. Schools—Fiction.
5. Mice—Fiction.]   I. Title.   PZ7.H389Wg
2000   [E]—dc21   99-34341   CIP

2 3 4 5 6 7 8 9 10   First Edition

Wemberly worried about everything.

Big things,

I WANTED
TO MAKE SURE
YOU WERE
STILL HERE.

little things,

and things in between.

Wemberly worried in the morning.

She worried at night.

And she worried throughout the day.

"You worry too much," said her mother.

"When you worry, I worry," said her father.

"Worry, worry, worry," said her grandmother.

"Too much worry."

At home, Wemberly worried

about the tree in the front yard,

WHAT IF IT FALLS ON OUR HOUSE?

and the crack

in the living room wall,

and the noise the radiators made.

At the playground, Wemberly worried about

the chains on the swings,

and the bolts on the slide,

and the bars on the jungle gym.

And always, she worried about her doll, Petal.

"Don't worry," said her mother.

"Don't worry," said her father.

But Wemberly worried.

She worried and worried and worried.

When Wemberly was especially worried, she rubbed Petal's ears.

Wemberly worried that if she didn't stop worrying,

Petal would have no ears left at all.

On her birthday, Wemberly worried

that no one would come to her party.

"See," said her mother, "there was nothing to worry about."

But then Wemberly worried that there wouldn't be enough cake.

On Halloween, Wemberly worried

that there would be too many

butterflies in the neighborhood parade.

"See," said her father, "there was nothing to worry about."

But then Wemberly worried because she was the only one.

"You worry too much," said her mother.

"When you worry, I worry," said her father.

"Worry, worry, worry," said her grandmother.

"Too much worry."

Soon, Wemberly had a new worry: school.

Wemberly worried about the start of school

more than anything she had ever worried about before.

By the time the first day arrived, Wemberly had a long list of worries.

What if no one else has spots?

What if no one else wears stripes?

What if no one else brings a doll?

What if the teacher is mean?

What if the room smells bad?

What if they
make fun
of my name?

What if I can't
find the bathroom?

What if I hate
the snack?

What if
I have
to cry?

"Don't worry," said her mother.

"Don't worry," said her father.

But Wemberly worried.

She worried and worried and worried.

She worried all the way there.

HAVE FUN!

While Wemberly's parents talked to the teacher, Mrs. Peachum,

Wemberly looked around the room.

Then Mrs. Peachum said, "Wemberly, there is someone

I think you should meet."

Her name was Jewel.

She was standing by herself.

She was wearing stripes.

She was holding a doll.

At first, Wemberly and Jewel just peeked at each other.

"This is Petal," said Wemberly.

"This is Nibblet," said Jewel.

Petal waved.

Nibblet waved back.

"Hi," said Petal.

"Hi," said Nibblet.

"I rub her ears," said Wemberly.

"I rub her nose," said Jewel.

Throughout the morning, Wemberly and Jewel

sat side by side and played together whenever they could.

Petal and Nibblet sat side by side, too.

Wemberly worried.

But no more than usual.

And sometimes even less.

Before Wemberly knew it,

it was time to go home.

"Come back tomorrow," called Mrs. Peachum,

as the students walked out the door.

Wemberly turned and smiled and waved.

"I will," she said. "Don't worry."